First published in Great Britain by HarperCollins Publishers Ltd in 1996. ISBN 0 00 198150 1 (hardback) 10 9 8 7 6 5 4 3 2 1
ISBN 0 00 664541 0 (paperback) 10 9 8 7 6 5 4 3 2 1 Text and illustrations copyright © Ian Beck 1996
of HarperCollins Publishers Ltd, 77-85 Fulham Palace Road, Hammersmith, London W6 8JB. Printed and bound in Italy.

POPPY AND PIP'S BEDTIME

Ian Beck

Collins

An Imprint of HarperCollins*Publishers*

The moon was high in the sky.
It was Poppy and Pip's bedtime.

"Let's get ready," said Poppy.

Poppy changed into her pyjamas.
Pip checked that all was well.

Poppy brushed her teeth and Pip
shook his coat.
"Into bed, Pip,"
said Poppy.
"Wooof," yawned Pip.
Off went the light.

"Woof, woof, woof!"
On went the light.

"What is it, Pip?" said Poppy.
Pip had lost his toy.

They looked everywhere for
Pip's toy. In the cupboard...
In the toy box...

In the dresser...
And behind the door.

"Not here, Pip," said Poppy.
"Grrooof," said Pip.

Tap. Tap. Tap.

"Who's at the door?" said Poppy.
"Quack!" said a voice.
The little duck had lost her toy.

Poppy, Pip and the little duck
started to hunt for the lost toys.

Scratch. Scratch. Scratch.

"Who's at the door?" said Poppy.
"Miaow!" said a voice.
The little kitten had lost his toy.

Poppy, Pip, the duck and the kitten
started to hunt for all the toys.

"Quaaack!" said the little duck.

She had found the kitten's toy.

"Miaow, thank you,"
said the little kitten.

"Miaooww!"
said the little kitten.

He had found the little duck's toy.

"Quack, thank you,"
said the little duck.

"Woooof," said Pip sadly.

"Never mind Pip," said
Poppy, "you can have
my toy tonight."

But when she went to
fetch her toy, she
found Pip's
teddy under
her pillow!

Now everyone was happy.
"Come on," said Poppy, "it's time
you all went home to bed."

Goodnight, sleep tight.

Make friends with the
Collins **Toddler** stories

OUR BABY
Tony Bradman • Lynn Breeze

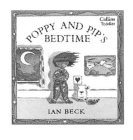

POPPY AND PIP'S BEDTIME
IAN BECK

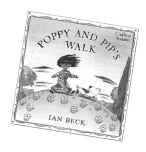

POPPY AND PIP'S WALK
IAN BECK

Teddy and Rabbit's Runaway Washing
Mark Burgess

Teddy and Rabbit's Picnic Outing
Mark Burgess

My Perfect Pet
Rachel Pank

Little Big Sister
Rachel Pank

The Bears Picnic
Andy Ellis

Foxy loses his tail
Colin and Jacqui Hawkins

Foxy goes to bed
Colin and Jacqui Hawkins